THE MYSTERY OF THE TALKING

TAIL

MARGARET CLARK

Illustrated by Bettina Guthridge

D1249324

sundance™

A Haights Cross Communications ® Company

Published by
Sundance Publishing
P.O.Box 740
One Beeman Road
Northborough, MA 01532
800-343-8204
www.sundancepub.com

Copyright © text Margaret Clark
Copyright © illustrations Bettina Guthridge
Project commissioned and managed by
Lorraine Bambrough-Kelly, The Writer's Style
Cover and text design by Marta White

First published 1996 by
Addison Wesley Longman Australia Pty Limited
95 Coventry Street
South Melbourne 3205 Australia
Exclusive United States Distribution: Sundance Publishing

ISBN-13: 978-0-7608-4958-3
ISBN-10: 0-7608-4958-7

Printed in China

Contents

CHAPTER 1

Bad Tempered

James was walking down the street when he found a tail.

at last...

"At last," said the tail. "I thought no one would ever come."

James stared at it in surprise.

A talking tail? It had to be a trick.
Carefully he bent down and looked closely at it.

"Don't you know
it's rude to stare?"
said the tail.

It was a most attractive tail, thick and bushy, very dark brown and furry, and quite long.

"Well, don't just leave me here. Pick me up," said the tail, wiggling on the path.

So James picked it up. It was very soft and very warm, as if it had just fallen off somebody. Or something.

"Ah. Would you like me to be *your* tail?" said the tail hopefully. It wound itself around James' arm invitingly.

James thought about it. A tail?
What would he do with it?
No other boys had tails.
Everyone would laugh at him.
His mother would be mad.

His brother would pull it, and his little sister would scream and yell and want one, too.

And his teacher would go off the planet.

"I don't really need a tail today," said James politely. "Anyway, what were you doing on the path? Are you lost?"

"No. I was sunbathing,"
said the tail in a very
angry voice.

"Don't be stupid, boy. Of course I'm lost,
otherwise I'd be attached, wouldn't I?"

James had to admit that the tail was right. Tails are always attached, dangling behind, or held straight up like his cat's tail when it was time for dinner, or swishing angrily like the one attached to a lion at the zoo.

This was definitely a lost tail. But what was he going to do with it?

"How did you get on the path?" James asked the tail.

"How do I know?" said the tail rudely.
"I woke up this morning lying on the path.
You're wasting time. Find my owner."

This was an extremely bad-tempered and ill-mannered tail. Maybe that was the reason its owner had made it drop off, thought James, putting the tail into his backpack.

He had to go to the store to buy a new pen on his way to school, so he didn't want everyone to see him wearing a tail like a big, furry bracelet.

"Who said that?" said the saleslady.

"That was *me*," said James. "I'm practicing to be a ventriloquist."

"Well, you were very good. I didn't even see your lips move at all," said the saleslady, smiling at James.

"Hey!" said the tail, but James stuffed it
back into his backpack with the pen and
held tightly to the end of the zipper so the
tail couldn't get out.

CHAPTER 2

Who'll Take This Tail?

James hurried to school. When it was time for the morning news he went up to the front of the class with his backpack.

"Your turn, James," said Mr. Patchett.

22

"I'm a ventriloquist and this is my talking dummy."

He held up the tail.

"Did you know you've got bad breath and hairy nostrils?" said the tail to Mr. Patchett.

All of the children laughed and Mr. Patchett turned red in the face.

"That will do, James. Put that tail back in your backpack. Or else throw it in the trash can."

"Aw, bag your head, suck your socks, and jump under a bus," said the tail.

Mr. Patchett lost it!

He went ape!

He made James go and sit at the back of the room in the corner and read quietly so he wouldn't disturb the others who were reading in groups.

James decided to show the tail some pictures in the books. Maybe it might recognize its owner!

At recess, James went off by himself with the tail in his backpack.

He *had* to find a home for the tail.

A dog came snuffling into the schoolyard, looking for food. It had a short, stubby tail.

'Would you like a nice, long tail?" James asked the dog.

He put the tail onto the dog and it stuck there, looking quite smart. The dog liked it. It wagged the tail furiously.

"Help!" said the tail, "I hate this. It's making me dizzy."

The tail dropped onto the ground and the dog ran off in fright.

"Well," said James, "maybe you'd like to be attached to a car antenna?"

He put the tail onto the antenna of Mr. Patchett's bright red car.

"Hey!" said the tail. "Dumb idea. I hate music."

The tail dropped onto the ground and wriggled sulkily.

James tried putting the tail on a little girl with very short hair.

"You look nice with a ponytail," he said to her.

"I'm not a ponytail!" yelled the tail angrily, swishing off the girl's head and back onto James' arm.

James was desperate.

He put the tail back in his backpack.

For the rest of the day the tail stayed in James' backpack. When he peeped in, it seemed to be asleep. James thought and thought.

Maybe it had escaped from a mad scientist?

Maybe it was an alien from a spaceship?

CHAPTER 3

Head of the Tails

At the end of the school day, James decided to take the tail to visit his granny.

Gran when she was YounG → (dinosauR dAYs!!)

She lived with a lot of grannies in the Eventide Retirement Home.

"Where are we going?" asked the tail, waking up and peering out of the backpack as James reached Granny's room.

"What on earth is that?" said Granny,
who was sitting in a chair by the window.

"A talking tail. I found it this morning
but I don't know what to do with it."

"Oh, aren't you the cutest thing?"
said Granny.
She cuddled the tail on her lap.

The tail made an odd rumbling noise.
"It's purring," said Granny as she stroked it.

She picked up the tail and wrapped it round her neck like a nice, warm scarf.

James followed Granny to the TV room where all the grannies were sitting in a long row gazing vacantly.

"Look," she said, "a beautiful talking tail."

All the grannies were excited.

"It reminds me of the fox-fur stole my first boyfriend gave me," said one granny, reaching for the tail.

What will we call it?

Furry?

Emmaline?

Sir Fur?

Thomas?

The tail squirmed with delight.
It liked "Sir Fur."

"But first," said James' granny, "we will have to advertise in the Lost and Found. Someone must be searching for this magnificent Sir Fur tail."

All the other grannies looked sad.
"Maybe nobody will claim Sir Fur,"
said James, so they all cheered up.

They put advertisements in all the papers.

But nobody claimed Sir Fur.

James was amazed. The tail stopped being so bad-tempered.

It told stories to the old grannies who couldn't see too well anymore.

It wrapped itself around their necks to keep them warm . . .

. . . or snuggled on their feet.

It rubbed their itchy backs.

It slept on their laps.

Sir Fur was so popular that the grannies all wanted to have the tail for themselves.

They started to fight and argue. Each one wanted it.

"It's mine," said James' granny. "My grandson gave it to me."

"But Granny, you told me it's good to share," said James.

And Sir Fur the tail swelled with pride.
All the attention was going to its head!

Then James had an idea.

He went to school the next day and explained his idea to Mr. Patchett.

"Great idea!" said Mr. Patchett, and he told the whole class.

"Fantastic idea!" said everyone.

And so they got busy.

When the children had made a big basket of fake-fur tails, they all piled into the school minibus and Mr. Patchett drove down the street to the Eventide Home for the Aged.

Each of them carried their favorite storybook

"Reckon she'll like *Space Ace*?"

"Mine is about ponies."

Sir Fur the tail was upset when he saw all the tails. *He* wanted to be the *only* tail.

"But you're the only *talking* tail," said James. "You are Head of the Tails."

So every granny had a tail and a child to
read to her.

They stroked their tails and felt happy.

And James made a roster for Story-telling
Time with the talking tail ...

... and a roster for neck-warming,
and foot-warming and back-rubbing,
so that Sir Fur was too busy to be grumpy.

So you can see that this tail has a very
happy ending!